WHAT DOES AN ANTEATER EAT?

For Ridley

First published 2018 by Nosy Crow Ltd
The Crow's Nest, 14 Baden Place
Crosby Row, London SE1 1YW
www.nosycrow.com

This edition published 2019

ISBN 978 1 78800 535 7

Nosy Crow and associated logos are trademarks
and/or registered trademarks of Nosy Crow Ltd

Text and illustrations © Ross Collins 2018

A CIP catalogue record for this book is available from the British Library.

Printed in China
Papers used by Nosy Crow are made from wood grown in
sustainable forests.

10 9 8 7 6 5 4 3 2 1

WHAT DOES AN ANTEATER EAT?

ROSS COLLINS

I'm hungry.

Good morning.
I know this sounds odd,
but do you happen to know
what an anteater eats?

I'm very busy. Don't bother me.

Ah. I see. I'm sorry
to have interrupted you.

Hello. I wonder, do you know
what an anteater eats?

Watermelon.

Watermelon? Really?
Are you sure?

Definitely watermelon. Trust me, I'm a melon expert.

I'm not completely convinced.

Excuse me. I don't suppose you know what an anteater eats, do you?

I'm sorry, I don't.
But I would really recommend
that you chew your food.

That's good advice.
Thank you.

Sorry to bother you.
You wouldn't happen to know
what an anteater eats,
would you?

I'm afraid not. But this old fish is delicious. Want to try some?

Thank you, but . . . no.

Hello.

I don't suppose you fellas happen to know what an anteater eats, do you?

I wonder if I might ask . . .
do you happen to know what
an anteater eats?

I'm afraid I don't,
but I must say –
you look very tasty . . .

Oh . . . I really must be going.

Excuse me.

I don't suppose you happen
to know what an . . .

I know what an anteater eats!

BANA

NAS !